RUTLAND MIDDLE SCHOOL LIBRARY
715 RUTLAND ROAD
KELOWNA, BC V1X 3B6
PHONE (250) 870-5109

M.Kayla Spence

To my future children and my nephew, Alac. I hope they, along with every other child in the world, grow up believing you're never limited by being a boy or girl. You're human and can do anything you set your minds to, you just have to put in the effort. I love you guys.

www.mascotbooks.com

The Prince S.

For more information, please contact:
Mascot Books
560 Herndon Parkway #120
Herndon, VA 20170
info@mascotbooks.com

Library of Congress Control Number: 2015915577

CPSIA Code: PRT1115A
ISBN-13: 978-1-63177-400-3

Printed in the United States

by **Mikayla Spence**   *Illustrated by* **Kathleen Joyce**

Once there was a young prince. He lived in a land not many people knew. He was a fine young man. As long as he could remember, he wished he were a princess. They were so beautiful, and he knew he could be just as pretty as them.

The king told him, "You can be anything you wish!" Well, if he wanted to be a princess, by golly he was going to do it!

So the prince set out to question the townspeople about what made a princess a princess. The prince stumbled upon a baker. He walked up to him and asked, "Sir, what makes a princess a princess?"

"Well, a princess should be sweet," replied the baker.

"How can I become sweet?"

"You can't be a sweet princess. Aren't you a boy?" the baker chuckled.

"Yes, but the king said I can be whatever I wish," explained the prince.

"Well then, take some of my favorite sweets. Perhaps they'll help."

"Why thank you, sir!
I would like to help you in return."

The prince helped the baker carry heavy flour bags inside.

The baker smiled at the prince as he danced away. *The boy is very sweet*, the baker thought.

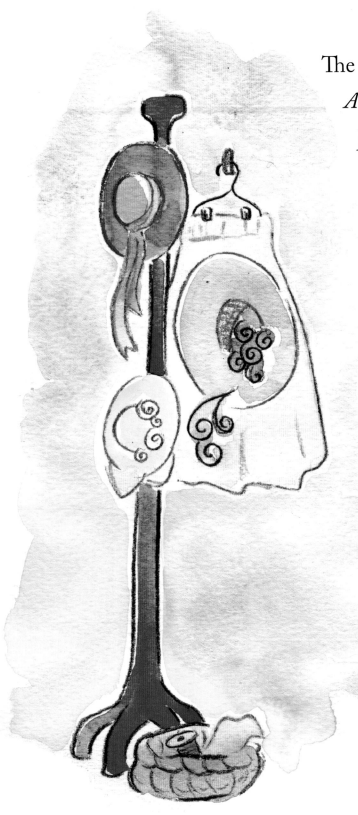

The prince soon came to a tailor. *A dress! That's what all pretty princesses need,* he thought. The prince asked the pretty lady at the counter, "Tailor, I wish to be a princess and need a pretty dress. Would you help me?"

"Why would you want to be a princess? You're such a handsome lad," the tailor wondered.

The prince looked at himself in the mirror and said, "I just know it's what I'm meant to be."

"Of course I'll help you!" she exclaimed.

She began furiously throwing fabrics in every direction.

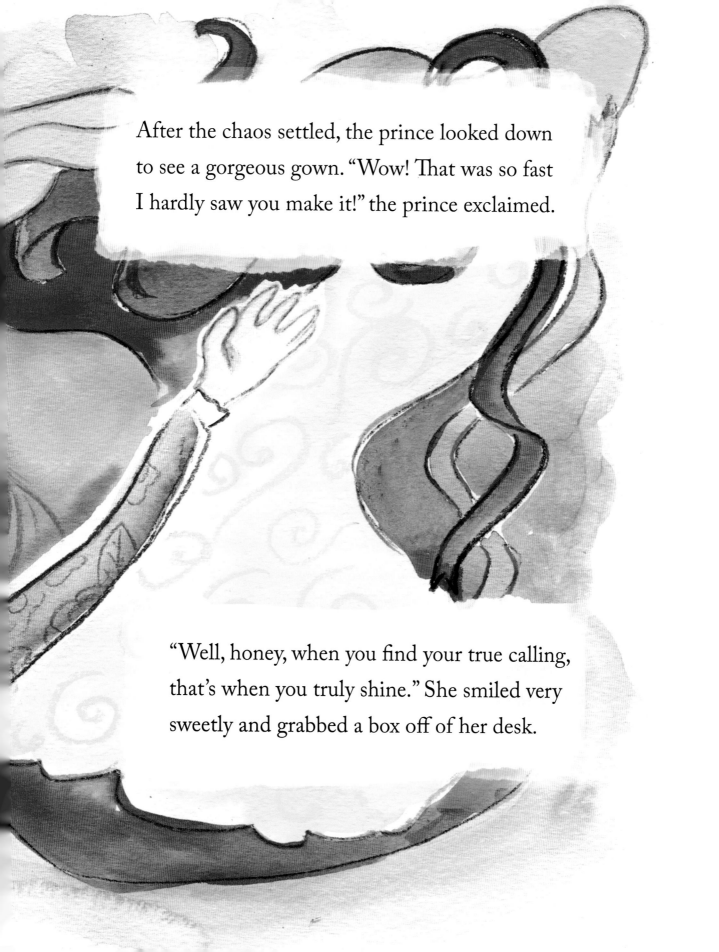

After the chaos settled, the prince looked down to see a gorgeous gown. "Wow! That was so fast I hardly saw you make it!" the prince exclaimed.

"Well, honey, when you find your true calling, that's when you truly shine." She smiled very sweetly and grabbed a box off of her desk.

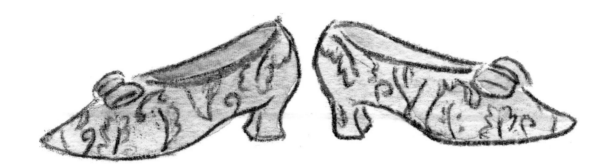

Inside was a pair of princess shoes that were made just for him. He slid them on his feet, grinning up at the tailor.

"Oh! One more thing before I send you off. Close your eyes!"

The prince did what was asked of him.

"Okay, look!"

He opened his eyes to see that she had released his hair from his ponytail. He looked to the mirror and yelled, "Wow!" The prince's eyes lit up. "Thank you so much."

As the tailor watched the prince skip
away she thought, *He's so much more beautiful
now that he's found his true calling.*

It was starting to get late. *Just one more stop,* he thought.

The prince's uncle, the blacksmith, was finishing a sword when he asked, "Uncle, I would like to be a princess. Is there anything I'm missing?"

"Well there, little buddy. You do look like a princess, that's for sure. A beautiful one too, if I may say so. I think the only thing missing is a princess crown. I may have the perfect one."

The blacksmith took the prince's crown, looped a rope around it, and tied it around the prince's waist.

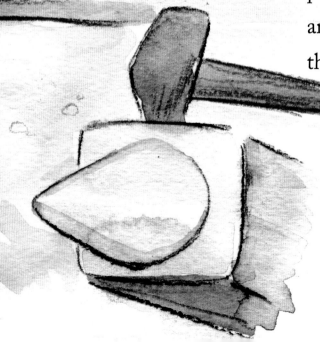

He then placed the princess crown on top of the prince's head.

The prince was speechless. This had been the most perfect day! Finally, he was a princess.

The prince walked home and snacked on his

sweets. *I'm so happy. I'm really a princess now!*

When he finally made it home, he went straight to his room

and plopped on the bed.

He was half asleep when there was a knock on his door. "Come in," he said.

The door opened to reveal the king who looked more than a little surprised. "What's going on here?" the king asked.

"Well, Dad, I wanted to be a princess so I became one. I know boys don't usually become princesses, but I think more should so they can all be as happy as me. I've been so happy today, everyone was so nice. It's been such a perfect day. I think I'd like to be a princess forever!" said the king's little prince.

"You can be and do anything you wish. So if you want to be a princess, you go for it! I'm very proud of you, and I love you no matter what. As long as you're happy, so am I." The king smiled, tucked his prince into bed, and kissed him goodnight.

The End

About the Author

Mikayla lives in Kelowna, Canada and really misses the cold Albertan weather. She has two cats Milky and Zelda, a dog Jeriko, and hamster Frankie. Mikayla is all finished with school but doesn't have any plans for the future as of yet. She loves her mom, dad, and sister very much.